Christmas

with

Princess Mirror-Belle

Books by Julia Donaldson
illustrated by Lydia Monks

The Princess Mirror-Belle series
Princess Mirror-Belle
Princess Mirror-Belle and the Magic Shoes
Princess Mirror-Belle and the Flying Horse
Christmas with Princess Mirror-Belle

Picture books
Princess Mirror-Belle and the Dragon Pox
The Princess and the Wizard
The Rhyming Rabbit
Sharing a Shell
The Singing Mermaid
Sugarlump and the Unicorn
What the Ladybird Heard
What the Ladybird Heard Next
What the Ladybird Heard on Holiday

Plays
The What the Ladybird Heard Play
The What the Ladybird Heard Next Play

★ JULIA DONALDSON ★

Christmas
with
Princess Mirror-Belle

Illustrated by
LYDIA MONKS

MACMILLAN CHILDREN'S BOOKS

'The Sleepwalking Beauty' first published 2006 in
Princess Mirror-Belle and the Flying Horse by Macmillan Children's Books
This edition published 2016 by Macmillan Children's Books

This edition reissued 2017 by Macmillan Children's Books
an imprint of Pan Macmillan
20 New Wharf Road, London N1 9RR
Associated companies throughout the world
www.panmacmillan.com

ISBN 978-1-5098-3892-9

1 3 5 7 9 8 6 4 2

A CIP catalogue record for this book is available from
the British Library.

Printed and bound by CPI Group (UK) Ltd, Croydon CR0 4YY

For Saoirse

Contents

Swan Lake 1

The Sleepwalking Beauty 41

Ellen and Mirror-Belle's
   Christmas Activities 81

Swan Lake

It was a Saturday morning in December, and Ellen was drinking a glass of hot lemon and honey at the kitchen table. When she'd finished it she tried to sing:

> "On the first day of Christmas, my
>   True Love gave to me
> A partridge in a pear tree.
> On the second day of Christmas . . ."

It was no use: her voice was coming out all croaky. Ellen had had a bad cold and, although she felt much better, her throat wasn't quite right yet. The lemon and honey drink hadn't really helped. That meant she almost certainly wouldn't be able to go out carol singing with her friends that night.

She tried one more time:

"On the seventh day of Christmas,
 my True Love gave to me
Seven swans a-swimming . . ."

"You sound more like a swan a-*dying*," said Ellen's big brother Luke, who was up early for once. (Usually he slept till lunchtime at weekends.) "Can't you stop that awful din?"

A dying swan! That reminded Ellen that she should be at her ballet class in ten minutes. They were rehearsing for their end-of-term show. It was going to be a children's version of the famous ballet *Swan Lake*. At least there was no singing in that.

In the ballet, Ellen was one of the maidens who had been turned into swans by a wicked sorcerer.

Ignoring Luke, she ran upstairs and hastily packed her swan costume into a bag. The costume was quite simple: just white tights and T-shirt and a headband with an orange beak and two black eyes stitched on it.

Even though Ellen took the shortcut

4

through the park, by the time she reached the hall where the ballet class was held, the changing room was empty. "I'm late again," she scolded herself. She hoped that Madame Jolie, the ballet teacher, wouldn't be cross. She put on her costume as quickly as possible, then checked in the mirror that the swan's beak was in the middle of the headband.

"Oh no – don't say the sorcerer turned *you* into a swan like me!" said her reflection. Except that of course it wasn't her reflection – it was Princess Mirror-Belle. She looked just like Ellen, but was very different in character.

"Mirror-Belle! What are you doing here? You know what happened last time."

Mirror-Belle had come to the ballet class once before, and Ellen didn't want her there again. That time Mirror-Belle had told everyone that her shoes were magic and wouldn't stop dancing. Madame Jolie was not at all impressed, and had ordered her to leave.

"Fear not!" said Mirror-Belle, springing out of the mirror. "I'm not wearing my magic shoes this time. They wore out. But I'm shocked to see you with that beak. I thought the sorcerer's magic only worked on princesses like me."

"It's not a real beak – and the sorcerer is just in a ballet," said Ellen. "Anyway, I can't stay and chat – I'm already late."

Turning her back on Mirror-Belle, she opened the door to the ballet room, hoping that Mirror-Belle wouldn't follow her.

The other pupils in the ballet class were standing in a line with their toes turned out. Almost all of them were wearing swan outfits like Ellen.

"I'm sorry I'm late, Madame," said Ellen in her croaky voice. But instead of telling her off, Madame Jolie fixed her attention on Mirror-Belle who had followed Ellen and was fluttering her arms behind her back like wings. Ellen expected the teacher to be furious, but instead Madame Jolie clapped her hands in delight.

"Yes! Yes! Zat is just ze movement I 'ave been trying to teach you all!" she said. "Everyone watch zees little newcomer and copy 'er. Arms back, fingers spread out, and *flutter*! Well done, my dear, you move just like a real swan."

"That's because I *am* one!" replied Mirror-Belle. "A wicked sorcerer turned me into one, and I see he's been at work here too. There's a whole flock of you!"

Madame Jolie laughed. She obviously didn't recognize Mirror-Belle as the girl who had once been so cheeky in her class. "Ah, you know already ze story," she said. "Zat is very good. Now, join ze line, please."

"It's not just a *story*," said Mirror-Belle. "It's only too real. Unless we can discover the spell to break the magic we'll all be swans for the rest of our lives."

"Zat is enough talking," said Madame Jolie. "Now, we will practise ze 'ead movements. Everyone, look to ze right, zen to ze left, and zen dip your 'eads as if you are looking down into ze lake. Imagine zat your necks are long, long, like real swans!"

Ellen and the others copied her – all except for Mirror-Belle. "I agree about not wasting time talking," she said. "There's no time to lose – we need to find the sorcerer and discover the spell, before every maiden in the world is turned into a swan."

Madame Jolie sighed. Her delight in her new pupil was wearing off, but she explained patiently, "We already 'ave a sorcerer." She pointed to a little boy with a black cloak and an innocent expression. "Oscar is doing a very good job," she said. "'E does ze dance very well; 'e just needs to practise looking more – 'ow do you say? – more evil."

"Nonsense!" said Mirror-Belle. "That's a mere child. The sorcerer is a fully grown man. We must go in search of him immediately." She pranced towards the door, flapping her arms wildly as if she were flying. "Are you coming with me, Ellen?" she asked.

Ellen shook her head and felt her face turn pink.

"What a strange child," said Madame Jolie once Mirror-Belle had gone. "She looks very like you, Ellen. Did you bring her?"

"No, Madame," said Ellen. She didn't feel like explaining how Mirror-Belle had come out of the mirror; no one ever believed her anyway.

"Well, never mind. We 'ave now wasted 'alf ze class. Let us practise ze scene when ze sorcerer comes back. Everyone, bend ze knees, raise ze arms and turn ze 'ead away from Oscar; remember, 'e is a wicked sorcerer and you are terrified of 'im. Oscar, please do not smile! You are evil, remember – evil!"

As the practice continued Ellen tried not to think about Mirror-Belle. When the class had finished they all curtsied to Madame Jolie and trooped into the changing room. Ellen was relieved that no one else was there; perhaps Mirror-Belle had gone back through the mirror to search for the sorcerer in her own world.

Ellen had another go at singing as she walked back through the park:

"On the third day of Christmas,
  my True Love sent to me
Three French hens . . ."

"That sounds terrible, Ellen," came a voice from behind a bush, and out popped Princess Mirror-Belle. She was still dressed in white and wearing the swan headband. "The sorcerer must have robbed you of your voice," she went on. "Swans can't sing, you know. Mind you, you don't look like a swan any more, which is strange. I wonder why that is. Maybe the magic didn't totally work on you because you're not a princess like me."

✳ 13 ✦

"Mirror-Belle, you look freezing. Do you want to borrow my coat?"

"Thank you, that would be very nice, even though it doesn't have any gold and silver embroidery like my one back home."

Mirror-Belle put the coat on, and it was Ellen's turn to feel cold, but she wound her scarf round a couple of extra times. "What are you doing here anyway?" she asked.

"Looking for the sorcerer, of course. I imagine he must live quite near a lake and someone told me there was one in this park."

"Yes – well, it's more of a duck pond really. Shall I show you?"

"Of course," said Mirror-Belle. "Lead on!"

They soon came to the pond, which had patches of ice on it. As well as the ducks, there were seven swans in the water – three white and four grey ones. Mirror-Belle gave a loud gasp. "It's Swan Lake!" she said.

"The grey ones are the cygnets – they'll turn white when they're fully grown," said Ellen.

"I very much hope not," said Mirror-Belle. "If my plan works, they'll all have turned back into maidens before then."

"No, these are real swans," said Ellen. "I've seen them loads of times. Sometimes we come and feed them."

But Mirror-Belle wasn't paying attention. Instead, she was fixing her gaze on a man with a broom who was walking towards them, sweeping the path. "There he is!" she whispered dramatically.

"Who?"

"The sorcerer!"

"Don't be silly – that's Mr Hollings. He looks after the park and does the gardening."

"Ellen, I despair of you sometimes. Can you *never* see through anyone's disguise? And have you not noticed his broomstick?"

It was true that the park-keeper's broom was the kind that looked like a witch's one, with a bundle of twigs tied on to the handle. "But lots of gardeners have brooms like that," said Ellen. "I think they're the best kind for sweeping up leaves."

"He's talking to himself," said Mirror-Belle.

"He always does that," said Ellen. "I think he's going over all the jobs he has to do."

"No, he's chanting a spell – I'm sure of it!" said Mirror-Belle.

Mr Hollings was quite near them by then. "Clean the tools, tidy the shed," they heard him mutter. Then he noticed them and raised his hand in a cheery greeting. "Hello, young ladies," he said. "The pond's freezing over. I hope we're not in for a cold spell."

Ellen expected Mirror-Belle to start accusing him of turning maidens into swans, but in fact she just glared at him and said nothing. Mr Hollings carried on past them, still sweeping.

"Did you hear that?" said Mirror-Belle when he was out of earshot. "He said something about a *spell* but he said he hoped it wouldn't happen. He must be talking about the spell to turn the swans back into maidens."

"Don't be silly," said Ellen. "He just meant that the weather was getting colder. And it is – I'm freezing. I need to get home."

"You can go where you like, Ellen, but I'm staying here. I'm going to find out what the spell is, and then I'm going to say it and set the maidens free."

"But what about my coat?" asked Ellen.

"I'll bring it back to you once I've found out the spell," said Mirror-Belle.

*

"Where's your coat?" asked Mum when Ellen arrived home.

"I lent it to Mirror-Belle," said Ellen.

"I do wish you wouldn't use that old excuse," said Mum, who thought that Princess Mirror-Belle was just an imaginary friend. "You must have left it at the ballet class."

She was about to tell Ellen to go back and fetch the coat, but just then the doorbell rang.

"That's probably her now," said Ellen.

But it wasn't; it was Robert Rumbold, one of Mum's piano pupils, who had come for his lesson. Mum showed him into the sitting room and soon Ellen could hear him thumping away at

 19

"O Little Town of Bethlehem".

The bell went three more times during the afternoon, but each time it was another piano pupil. As it began to grow dark, Ellen wondered what Mirror-Belle was up to. Was she still spying on Mr Hollings?

"I forgot to tell you, Ellen," said Mum when the last pupil had left, "Dad and I are going to a drinks do this evening. It's only for a couple of hours, but I'm afraid children aren't invited. Luke's out at his band practice, so I've asked Sara to come and babysit."

"Good," said Ellen. She liked Sara, who used to live next door. She had gone away to university but was back home for the Christmas holidays. Now Ellen wouldn't mind so much about being too croaky to go out carol-singing with her friends.

When Sara arrived she was keen to see Ellen practise her dancing, so Ellen got into her swan outfit and did a demonstration.

"The hardest part is when we all have to stand on one leg with the other toe touching our knee. It's meant to be how swans go to sleep, but I always wobble. I'm afraid I might fall over during the actual show."

"I'm sure you won't," said Sara. "I can show you a special way of keeping your balance—"

But she was interrupted by the doorbell. This time it *was* Mirror-Belle. She was still wearing Ellen's coat and the swan's-beak headband.

"I have some very important and highly

confidential information for Ellen," she announced.

Sara laughed. "I didn't know Ellen had a friend coming round," she said. "You must be another of the swans."

"That's right," said Mirror-Belle. "And I see that Ellen has been turned back into one too. But not for long!" She had a triumphant expression on her face and a piece of paper in her hand.

"Perhaps I'd just better phone your home to check they know you're here," said Sara. "What's your number?"

"I don't know what you mean," said Mirror-Belle. "Princesses have names, not numbers. I suppose if I did have one, it would be number one."

"No, I mean your telephone number."

"I don't think her family has a phone," said Ellen.

"If you want to send a message to my parents, the King and Queen, you could try strapping one on to the back of a turtle dove," said Mirror-Belle. "Though if your writing is backwards, like most people around here, I doubt if they'd be able to read it."

Sara looked a bit bewildered. "Well,

maybe it's all right if you're not staying for long," she said. "Have you just come to practise the dance with Ellen?"

"Yes," said Ellen quickly, and then, to Mirror-Belle, "Let's go up to my room."

Upstairs, Mirror-Belle held out the piece of paper she was carrying. "I'm hoping you can read this, Ellen. I went to a lot of trouble to obtain it. I followed the sorcerer round for absolutely hours."

"And what happened?" Even though Ellen didn't really believe that Mr Hollings was a sorcerer, she couldn't help being interested.

"He spent a long time fiddling about with his broomstick. I was afraid he might fly off on it, but in the end he put it into his den of evil."

"I suppose you mean his tool shed," said Ellen.

"You can call it what you like, Ellen, but the next thing he did was very sinister. He took out a sharp object and started to cut branches off the bushes."

"That's called pruning," said Ellen. "It keeps the bushes nice and healthy, and stops them getting too woody."

"I think it's far more likely that the branches had overheard his secrets and he wanted to make sure they didn't tell them to the wind."

Ellen decided not to argue. "What happened next?" she asked.

"Well, all the time he was muttering the words of the spell, but I couldn't get close enough to hear exactly what he was saying. But then he went back into his den and wrote it down! I could hardly believe my luck. Here it is!"

She waved the piece of paper at Ellen, who could see now that it had been torn out of a notebook.

"How did you get hold of it?" she asked.

"I was just coming to that," said Mirror-Belle. "After he'd finished writing, the

 sorcerer locked the door of the den and went away. But I noticed that there was a window, and that one of the panes was broken. So I stuck my arm in and managed to reach

his spell book. I tore out the last page and threw the book back on to his table. As I suspected, his writing is just as terrible as yours – all back to front. So I'm hoping you will be able to read it for me." She handed the paper to Ellen.

Mr Hollings's handwriting was a bit of a scrawl, but Ellen managed to read what was on the page:

"'Mend the broken windowpane
Clear the drain
Fix the fence
Prune the rose
Clean the tools
Repair the hose
Oil the swing.'

"It's just a list of jobs," she said.

"It *sounds* like that, I agree," said Mirror-Belle. "But that just shows how cunning he is. He's made up a spell that doesn't sound like a spell, so no one will suspect."

"But even if it was a spell, it would be one to turn people into swans, not to turn swans into people, wouldn't it?" said Ellen.

"Of course – but all we need to do is to say the spell the other way round, and that will undo the magic."

"What, read it backwards, do you mean?"

"Not exactly. Just read the last line first, and so on till we get to the top."

"Well, it can't do any harm, I suppose," said Ellen.

"Harm? Of course not! We'll be doing tremendous *good*! Can you write it out like that for us to chant?"

So Ellen wrote out the list in the opposite order, in her neatest handwriting. Then she found a little pocket mirror and gave it to Mirror-Belle to hold up against the paper. "Just read the writing in the mirror," she said, "and I'll read what's on the paper. That way it'll be easy for both of us."

"Thank you, Ellen," said Mirror-Belle, "though one of these days you really will have to learn to write properly. Now, are you ready? One, two, three, chant!"

Then together, the two girls read aloud:

"'Oil the swing
Repair the hose

Clean the tools
Prune the rose
Fix the fence
Clear the drain
Mend the broken windowpane.'"

"You see – it *rhymes*!" said Mirror-Belle. "That proves it's the right spell. And look!" She pulled the headband off her head. "I'm not a swan any more."

"But you could have done that at any time," said Ellen. "They come off easily –" And she removed her own headband.

"Hush! Can you hear the singing?" said Mirror-Belle.

Ellen listened. "Yes, I can."

The voices were coming from outside; faint but growing louder:

"On the fifth day of Christmas, my True
Love sent to me Five gold rings."

"It's worked!" cried Mirror-Belle.

"What do you mean?"

"It's the maidens singing. They've been
changed back!"

"I think it's my friends singing carols,"
said Ellen. "They'll probably come to our
house next."

The two girls looked out of the window.
The little troop of singers was coming up
the road, led by the singing teacher from
Ellen's school, Miss Bell. They stopped
outside the front door.

"Let's go down and listen properly," said
Ellen.

They ran downstairs. Sara had already

opened the front door and the three of them stood and listened to the carol.

"On the eighth day of Christmas, my
    True Love sent to me
Eight maids a-milking
Seven swans a-swimming –"

"You see!" said Mirror-Belle triumphantly. "The song is all about maidens and swans. That absolutely proves it!"

When the carol had finished, Miss Bell said, "Hello, Ellen. It's a shame you couldn't come with us." She was carrying a tin and she held it out. "We're collecting for a children's charity," she said.

"Why not Swans in Need?" asked Mirror-Belle.

Miss Bell laughed uncertainly. "I don't know much about swans, I'm afraid," she said.

"You must have escaped the sorcerer's spell then," said Mirror-Belle. "But I'm sure these other maidens know *all* about

swans. Ellen and I only set them free a few minutes ago."

"That's enough of that," said Sara, and she put some money into Miss Bell's collecting tin.

"They don't seem very grateful," muttered Mirror-Belle. Then, when the carol singers had gone, she announced, "I must go too. My parents will be worrying about me desperately."

"Oh dear – I thought they knew you were here," said Sara.

"No – they probably still think I'm swimming about on a lake," said Mirror-Belle. "Goodbye, Ellen!" And she ran upstairs.

"Has she gone to fetch something?" asked Sara.

"I'll go and see," said Ellen. But when she went into her bedroom there was no sign of Mirror-Belle. Ellen wasn't surprised. She saw that her coat was lying on the floor in front of the wall mirror, and she felt sure that Mirror-Belle must have gone back through the mirror into her own world.

Just then she heard a key in the door followed by voices in the hall. Her parents were back.

"They're both upstairs," Sara told them.

Mum came in. "Sara said you had a friend round," she said.

"Yes, but she's gone," said Ellen.

"Oh good, you've got your coat back." Mum picked it up. "But the sleeve is a bit torn. How did that happen?"

"It was Mirror-Belle – she caught it on a branch," said Ellen.

Mum sighed but decided not to get into a conversation about Mirror-Belle. "Well, it was getting a bit small for you anyway," she said.

Madame Jolie beamed as she pirouetted on to the stage. The performance of *Swan Lake* had just finished and the audience was clapping and clapping.

The ballet had gone really well. Ellen hadn't wobbled, and Oscar had managed not to smile once. At last the applause died down and Madame Jolie made a little speech.

"Thank you, thank you, everyone. Thank you to all ze parents and grandparents for coming tonight, and a very big thank you to all ze children who 'ave been dancing so well. Now we will 'ave ze tea, coffee and some very special biscuits. I 'ope zat you will all stay."

The biscuits were shaped like swans and were covered in white icing.

"We'd better eat them up quick, or they might turn back into maidens," joked Ellen's dad.

"Well done, Ellen," said Mum. "And I must congratulate Oscar."

Oscar was standing nearby with his parents,

and Ellen was surprised when she saw who his father was. It was Mr Hollings, wearing a smart suit and looking quite different from how he did in the park. They were chatting to Madame Jolie. Mum went up to them. "Congratulations, Oscar," she said. "You were a wonderful villain."

"Yes, 'e looked evil – evil!" agreed Madame Jolie. "But always in ze rehearsals 'e was so smiley – I could not get 'im to frown and to look like ze baddy. 'Ow did you manage it, Oscar?"

"My dad helped me," said Oscar.

Ellen couldn't help smiling. She half wished that Mirror-Belle could be there. If she had been, Ellen knew exactly what she would say: "That proves it!"

The Sleepwalking Beauty

Christmas pudding or Sleeping Beauty? That was the question Ellen was asking herself as she wrapped up a present for her best friend Katy.

It was Christmas Eve, and Katy was having a fancy dress party. Ellen couldn't decide what to go as. She had already worn the Christmas pudding costume in the end-of-term ballet show. It had a wire frame which was quite uncomfortable and meant you couldn't sit down. Still, it did look good, especially the little cap with the sprig of holly on it.

The Sleeping Beauty costume wasn't so Christmassy. It was just a lacy white Victorian nightdress Ellen's mother had bought at a car-boot sale. But it was very pretty, and Ellen decided to wear it if she could find something else to go with it.

As soon as she had finished wrapping up the present she tried on the nightdress. Looking through her dressing-up box she found an old net curtain which she draped over her head. She fixed it into place with a gold-coloured plastic headband which looked quite like a crown. There was a pair of very long white button-up gloves in the box too. Mum had told her that her great-grandmother used to wear them for going to balls. Ellen put them on and then went to see how the whole outfit looked in her wardrobe mirror.

She should have known better, of course.

"I don't see why you need to bother with gloves," said Princess Mirror-Belle, looking at her critically from the mirror. "After all, what would it matter if you pricked your finger?"

Ellen was dismayed. "Oh, Mirror-Belle, this isn't a good time to come!" she said.

"What do you mean?" said Mirror-Belle, looking offended. "Surely you'd rather play with a princess than by yourself?"

"But I'm not going to be by myself. I'm just off to Katy's party. This is my Sleeping Beauty costume."

Mirror-Belle laughed. "Poor you, having to dress up as a Sleeping Beauty, when I really am one," she said.

"No you're not – you're Mirror-Belle."

"Of course – and 'Belle' means 'Beauty'. I thought everyone knew that. Have you forgotten what I told you the very first time we met?"

Ellen thought back. She did seem to remember some story about Mirror-Belle's wicked fairy godmother pricking her finger and sending her to sleep for a very long time. But then Mirror-Belle was always telling her stories and Ellen never knew how many of them were true.

Mirror-Belle had stepped out of the mirror and was looking round Ellen's bedroom. Her eyes fell on the cap belonging to the Christmas pudding costume.

"It's very careless of you to leave that holly lying around," she said. "Suppose I pricked my finger on it?"

"It's not real holly," said Ellen. "It's just made of plastic. And I don't know what you're so worried about. I thought you'd already gone to sleep for a hundred years."

"Two hundred," Mirror-Belle corrected her. "So what?"

"Well, you woke up in the end, didn't you? So the spell must be broken."

"You obviously don't know my wicked fairy godmother," said Mirror-Belle. "I'm in danger every day of my life. The next time I prick my finger it's going to happen all over again, only this time it could be for three hundred years. That's why I always wear gloves."

Ellen was sure she hadn't ever seen Mirror-Belle wearing gloves before, but she didn't want to start arguing about that now. "Well, anyway, Mirror-Belle, the party will be starting soon. I'll have to go."

"Don't you mean 'We'?" asked Mirror-Belle, looking offended again.

"No, I don't. I'm sorry, but it would all

be too complicated. Everyone would keep thinking you were me, or my twin or something, and I'm just not in the mood for that."

"Aha!" Mirror-Belle flipped her net curtain over her head so that it hid her face like a veil. "Now all your problems are solved!" she said.

Ellen doubted it, but she realized she couldn't win. "Oh, all right then. But we can't both wear the same costume. I'll have to be a Christmas pudding after all."

Ellen put her finger to her lips as they went downstairs. Mum had invited some of her piano pupils round to play Christmas carols to each other, and at the moment Robert Rumbold was hammering out

"Silent Night", though it sounded more like "Very Loud Night".

Katy's house was just round the corner. Her dad opened the door to Ellen and Mirror-Belle.

"Oh good, the food's arrived," he joked when he saw Ellen dressed as a Christmas pudding. "I hope they put a lot of brandy in you." He turned to Mirror-Belle. "And I suppose this delicious-looking white creation is the Christmas cake."

Ellen laughed politely, and then blushed when Mirror-Belle said in a haughty voice, "Please tell the lady of the house that the royal guest has arrived." She seemed to think that she was speaking to the butler.

Luckily Katy's father thought this was a great joke. "Katy! The princess and the pudding are here!" he called out. Then, "If you'll excuse me, I'd better pop upstairs and get changed," he said to Ellen and Mirror-Belle.

"Yes, you do look a bit scruffy. And don't forget to give your shoes a polish while you're at it," said Mirror-Belle.

Before Ellen could tick her off, Katy arrived, dressed as a reindeer.

"I've brought Mirror-Belle with me. I hope that's all right," said Ellen.

"Of course it is." Katy had already met Mirror-Belle once, when she had appeared at their school, and looked pleased to see her again. She took them both into the sitting room, where various children in fancy dress were chattering and eating crisps.

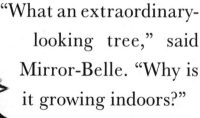

"What an extraordinary-looking tree," said Mirror-Belle. "Why is it growing indoors?"

"It's a Christmas tree," said Ellen.

Mirror-Belle was still bewildered. "What is this Christmas thing that everyone keeps talking about? Is it some kind of disease?"

Katy laughed. "No, of course not. Why do you think that?"

"Well, that tree looks diseased to me. Half the needles have fallen off it, and the fruits are gleaming in a most unhealthy-looking way. I think you should take it back to the forest immediately."

"They're not fruits, they're fairy lights," said Ellen.

"I think I'm the expert on fairies round here, and I've never heard of such a thing," said Mirror-Belle.

Katy's mother came in. "There's just time for one game before tea," she said.

She handed out pencils and paper and then showed them all a bag. "There are five different things inside here. You'll all get a turn to feel them and then write down what you think they are."

"I can't possibly risk that," objected Mirror-Belle. "Supposing there's something sharp in there? I might prick my finger. But I like the idea of tea. Perhaps you could call one of your servants and ask them to bring me mine while the rest of you play this game."

Katy's mother told her that she would have to wait and have tea with the others.

"But I promise you there's nothing sharp in the bag. Why don't you join in?"

Reluctantly Mirror-Belle agreed, though she refused to take her gloves off.

"This is easy," she said when it was her turn to feel inside the bag, and she began writing furiously.

"You can read out your list first if you like, Mirror-Belle," said Katy's mother when everyone was ready.

"Very well," said Mirror-Belle. "There's some mermaid's hair, a wishing ring, an invisibility pill, a witch's eyeball and a tool for removing stones from a unicorn's hoof."

Everyone laughed.

"Very imaginative," said Katy's mum. "I'll give you a mark for the pill, though I don't think it has any magic powers."

Ellen had written, "seaweed, ring pull from drink can, pill, grape and matchstick", and was delighted to find that she was the only one to get them all right. Her prize was a little snowman made out of meringue.

At teatime there were crackers to pull. Mirror-Belle refused to put on the paper crown inside hers and told everyone about the different crowns she had back home.

"Why are you wearing that veil thing?" someone asked.

"It's because my face is so beautiful that you might fall down dead if you saw it," replied Mirror-Belle. Then she kept them entertained with stories about life in the palace. Ellen was glad that the other children seemed to like Mirror-Belle and think she was fun.

It was after tea that the trouble started. When everyone was back in the sitting room, Katy's mother peeped out the door and announced, "He's coming!"

"Ho ho ho!" came a loud laugh and in strode Father Christmas. Ellen felt quite excited, even though Katy had told her that it was really just her dad dressed up.

"Merry Christmas, boys and girls!" said Father Christmas. "Happy holidays! Ho ho ho!"

"You're extremely late," Mirror-Belle told him. "All the food's gone already."

"Ho ho ho!" laughed Father Christmas, even louder than before.

"What's so funny?" asked Mirror-Belle.

Father Christmas took no notice of her. Still laughing, he heaved the sack off his back. "It's nice to see you all so wide awake!" he told the children. "When I come down your chimneys you're always fast asleep. It gets a bit lonely sometimes."

Mirror-Belle looked even more puzzled. "What do you mean, you come down chimneys? I hope you're not a burglar. We had one of those at the palace once. He stole all the crown jewels. But I chased him on my flying horse, Little Lord Lightning, and I got them back."

"Ho ho ho!" went Father Christmas, and one or two of the children laughed, but the others said "Shh" or "Shut up".

"Now then." Father Christmas took a present out of his sack. "Who's been good all year?" he asked.

"Me!" everyone shouted.

He beckoned to a girl dressed as a star and she came shyly forward.

"You look a bit of a star! Ho ho ho!"

Father Christmas handed her the present and she unwrapped it. It was a box of soaps shaped like bells.

"Thank you," said the star girl.

Ellen glanced at Mirror-Belle. She was still looking suspicious.

Father Christmas gave a torch to a boy dressed as a cracker, and a card game to one in a Batman costume.

"Excuse me, but are you quite sure these things are yours to give away?" Mirror-Belle asked him.

57

"Ho ho ho," replied Father Christmas, but Ellen didn't think he sounded quite so jolly as before. He beckoned to Mirror-Belle, perhaps hoping that once she had a present of her own she would stop pestering him.

"Now then, Your Royal Highness, let's find something special for you," he said.

Mirror-Belle gave him half a smile. "At least you know how to address me," she said. But when she opened her present her face fell.

"What are these supposed to be?" she asked, looking at the five little felt objects she had unwrapped.

Father Christmas didn't look too sure himself, so Ellen came to the rescue. "They're finger puppets," she said. "A reindeer and a robin and a snowman and a Christmas tree and Father Christmas. They're lovely, aren't they, Mirror-Belle?"

But Mirror-Belle didn't think so. "Is this a trick to get me to take off my gloves?" she asked Father Christmas. "Well, I'm not going to, but I think you should take off your socks and shoes."

"Mirror-Belle! Stop it!" said Ellen, but the Batman boy was intrigued. "Why should he?" he asked.

"They're stolen!" said Mirror-Belle. "They belong to the butler who opened the door."

"There isn't a butler," said someone, and, "She means Katy's dad," said someone else.

"Well, whoever he was, he was wearing

59

scruffy black shoes and socks with green-and-brown diamonds up the sides. Don't you remember, Ellen?" said Mirror-Belle.

"Now, now, you've had your bit of fun," said Father Christmas, covering up his shoes with the hem of his robe and trying to sound jolly again. "Let someone else have a turn, eh? Ho ho ho!"

But Mirror-Belle ignored him. "I see it all now!" she said. "The butler person told Ellen and me he was going upstairs to get changed, and I ordered him to polish his shabby shoes. He must have taken them off, and his socks too. Then I suppose he must have had a little nap, and meanwhile this burglar came down the chimney and stole them."

She turned to Katy's mother. "Aren't

you going to phone the police?"

"No," said Katy's mother, "but I think perhaps we'd better phone your parents and tell them you're getting a bit too excited."

"Of course I'm excited!" cried Mirror-Belle. "It's not every day you catch a crook red-handed. Look! He's even got a false beard!" She reached out and tried to tug it, but Father Christmas dodged out of the way.

"Now now, I'm beginning to wonder if you really are a good little girl," he said. "Maybe I'd better fill your stocking with coal instead of presents?"

Mirror-Belle looked horrified. "You're not filling any of my stockings with anything!" she said. "In fact, if you come anywhere near the palace I'll set my dog, Prince Precious Paws, on you. And you'd better not try going down my friend Ellen's chimney either."

"Of course I'll go down Ellen's chimney; she's a good girl, and I've got a little something for her here," said Father Christmas, beckoning to Ellen.

Ellen came up to receive her present. "Do calm down, Mirror-Belle," she pleaded.

"I know!" said Katy. "We're going to play hide-and-seek next. Why don't you go and hide now, Mirror-Belle? I bet you'll find a really good place."

Mirror-Belle sighed. "Very well, since no one here will listen to reason," she said, and she flounced out of the room.

Later, when all the presents had been

given out and Father Christmas had said goodbye, the other children went to look for Mirror-Belle. Ellen was not surprised when they couldn't find her.

"It's all right," she told Katy's mum. "I think she must have gone home. She quite often does that." She didn't add that the way Mirror-Belle went home was through a mirror.

Ellen thought she would never get to sleep. Christmas Eve was always like that. Her empty stocking (really one of Dad's thick mountain-climbing socks) lay limply on the bottom

of her bed. In the morning it would be fat and knobbly with presents, and this was just one of the exciting thoughts that was keeping her awake.

"But I did get to sleep all the other years, so I will tonight," she told herself, and in the end she must have drifted off.

A rapping sound woke her and she sat up in bed. The room was dark. It was still night.

She wriggled her toes. Yes! From the lovely heaviness on top of them she knew that her stocking was full. But why was her heart thumping so hard? It didn't feel just like nice Christmassy excitement. That noise had scared her. What was it?

Mum and Dad liked Ellen to take her

stocking into their room, so that they could watch her open it. This year she had decided to take them in a cup of tea as well. But somehow she knew it was too early for that. She switched on her lamp and looked at the clock beside her bed. Only four thirty.

Suddenly she heard another rap. It was coming from the skylight window. Ellen wished now that Mirror-Belle hadn't gone on about burglars so much, because that was the first thing she thought of. It sounded as if someone was trying to break into her bedroom.

"Ellen! Let me in!"

That hoarse whisper didn't belong to a burglar. It was Princess Mirror-Belle.

For once Ellen was relieved to see

her face, which was pressed against the skylight window.

"I'm coming!" she said and got out of bed.

The window was in the sloping part of Ellen's ceiling, where it came down so low that grown-ups couldn't stand up properly. Ellen didn't even need to climb on a chair to open it.

Princess Mirror-Belle landed on the floor with a thump. She didn't look much like Sleeping Beauty any more. Her face was dirty, her hair wild and her nightdress torn. In one hand she clutched the now grubby veil.

"Mirror-Belle! I thought you'd gone back through one of Katy's mirrors!"

"What, and leave you unprotected? Is that the kind of friend you think I am?"

"I don't know what you mean. Oh, Mirror-Belle, you're shivering! Why don't you get into my bed?"

"That's a good idea."

When the two girls were sitting up in bed together, snugly covered by Ellen's duvet, Ellen said, "What were you doing on the roof? And how did you get there?"

"I climbed up that creeper at the side of your house. Very useful things, creepers. I'm sure my friend Rapunzel wishes that there had been one growing up the tower that horrible witch locked her up in for all those years. Then the prince could have climbed up that instead of up her hair. I must say, I wouldn't let any old prince climb up my hair, even if it was long enough. A lot of Rapunzel's hair fell out after that, you know, and it's never been the same since."

"Oh, Mirror-Belle, do stop going on about Rapunzel and tell me what you've been up to."

"This," said Mirror-Belle, and she spread out the grubby veil which she had been clutching. Something was written on it in big black letters.

"I had to use a lump of coal for the writing, but it looks quite good, I think. Don't you?"

Ellen had become an expert at reading Mirror-Belle's writing so she didn't need to hold it up to the mirror to see that it said, "Go Away, Father Christmas."

"I spread it out on the roof and sat on the chimney pot all night," said Mirror-Belle triumphantly. "I'm pretty sure that's done the trick. I don't think he'll come now."

"Er . . ." Ellen couldn't help glancing down at the bulgy stocking on her bed, and Mirror-Belle spotted it too.

"Good heavens! He's craftier than I thought. How on earth did he get in? You'd better check all your belongings immediately, Ellen, and see what he's stolen."

"I'm sure he hasn't stolen anything," said Ellen.

Mirror-Belle glanced round the room suspiciously and then at the stocking again.

"I notice there isn't one for me," she said. "That's a relief," she added, though in fact she sounded rather disappointed.

Ellen thought quickly and then said, "I've got something for you, Mirror-Belle. Close your eyes a minute."

Mirror-Belle looked pleased, and Ellen hastily wrapped up the present that Father Christmas had given her at Katy's party.

"You can open them again now."

Mirror-Belle unwrapped the present, and gazed in delight at the little glass dome with a forest scene of deer and trees inside it.

"Give it a shake," said Ellen. Mirror-Belle shook it, and

snowflakes rose up and whirled around.

"This is just what I've always wanted," she said. Ellen had never heard her sound so happy about anything before and felt glad she had thought of giving her the snowstorm, even though she really liked it herself.

After a few more shakes and smiles, Mirror-Belle started eyeing Ellen's stocking again. "I hope it isn't full of coal," she said.

"I'm sure it's not."

"Let's just check."

"But I usually open it in Mum and Dad's room, and it's too early to wake them."

"I still think we have a duty to investigate," said Mirror-Belle grandly.

"Well . . ." Ellen was beginning to waver.

After all, it was so hard to wait. "I know, let's just open one thing each and then wrap them up again."

She gave Mirror-Belle a cube-shaped parcel and unwrapped a long thin one herself.

"Cool! It's a fan. What's in yours?"

"It's a little box." Mirror-Belle opened it and inside was a brooch shaped like a Scottie dog. "Hmm, not a patch on any of my own jewellery, but quite amusing all the same," she said. "Would you like me to fasten it on to your pyjama top?"

"Yes, please," said Ellen.

Suddenly Mirror-Belle gave a little scream.

"What's the matter?"

"I've pricked my finger!"

"Oh dear." Ellen looked at the finger which was sticking out of a hole in the dirty white glove. She couldn't see any blood or even a pinprick. "I'm sure you'll be all right," she said.

"No, I won't. I feel sleepy already."

"Oh help! Is there anything I can do?"

"No, nothing at all, but don't worry. It's quite a nice feeling actually. In fact, I think I probably *need* a three-hundred-year sleep after all the adventures I've had recently."

Mirror-Belle gave a huge yawn and lay down in Ellen's bed.

"No! You can't go to sleep here!"

But Mirror-Belle's eyes were already closed, and she began to snore gently.

"Wake up, Mirror-Belle!" Ellen was shouting now.

"Ellen! What's going on!" she heard her mother's voice call.

Ellen looked at the clock. It was half past five – still a bit earlier than her parents liked to be disturbed, but it seemed that she had woken them up already.

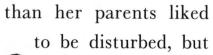

Well, she decided, at least now she could prove to them once and for all that Mirror-Belle really existed. If she was going to stay asleep in Ellen's bed for three hundred years there could be no doubt about that.

"Happy Christmas," said Mum sleepily, and then, "Oh, how lovely," when she saw that Ellen had brought her and Dad a cup of tea.

"Where's your stocking?" asked Dad.

"It's upstairs still, and so is Mirror-Belle! You've got to come and see her."

Mum sighed. "Honestly, Ellen, can't we even get a break from Mirror-Belle on Christmas Day?"

"But she's asleep in my bed! Please, Mum – please come!"

Mum yawned. "Let us drink our tea first," she said. "You go back up and we'll come in a couple of minutes."

"All right." After all, Ellen thought, there was no hurry.

But when she got back to her bedroom she found that Mirror-Belle was no longer in the bed. She was walking slowly across the room with her arms stretched out in front of her.

"Mirror-Belle! Have you woken up already?"

"No, of course not, silly. I'm sleep-walking," said Mirror-Belle. Ellen noticed that she was grasping the snowstorm in her right hand. She had reached the wardrobe now.

"Goodbye, Ellen," she said in a strange calm voice and disappeared into the mirror.

"Mirror-Belle! Come back!" Ellen

called into the mirror, but it was her own reflection and not Mirror-Belle that she saw there.

"All right then, where's this sleeping princess?" said Dad, coming into the room with Mum.

"You've just missed her," said Ellen. "She's sleepwalked into the mirror."

"Well, well, what a surprise," said Mum. Then she glanced at the wrapping paper on the bed. "I see you couldn't wait to start opening your stocking."

"That was Mirror-Belle's idea," said Ellen.

Mum smiled. "Of course," she said.

Ellen knew that Mum and Dad didn't believe her. It was annoying, but she didn't really blame them. There were quite a few

things about Mirror-Belle that she wasn't
sure if she believed herself. For instance,
had she really gone to sleep for three
hundred years? If so, Ellen would never
see her again – unless she did some more
sleepwalking, that is.

"Well," said Mum, "are you going to bring your stocking downstairs now?"

"Yes," said Ellen. Suddenly she felt excited all over again.

Mirror-Belle had gone, but Christmas Day had only just begun.

Ellen

and

Mirror-Belle's

Christmas Activities

Christmas Snowstorm

You will need
A screw-top jar
A small plastic toy – you could use
    some Christmas-cake decorations
Glycerine
Glue – not water-soluble . . .
and the special ingredient – some
    glitter!

1. Fill your jar with water and screw the lid on.
2. Now shake it about to make sure there aren't any leaks.
3. Empty the jar and refill it, using two parts water and one part glycerine. (The glycerine thickens the water so

that your glitter snow will fall slowly.)
Now sprinkle in the glitter and give it
a good stir.

4. Finally, glue your toy to the inside of
the lid and put the lid on tightly. Get
shaking – and admire your winter
wonderland!

Salt-Dough Tree Decorations

Your Christmas tree will look great covered with these non-edible decorations.

You will need
300g plain flour
300g salt
200ml water
1 teaspoon cooking oil
A rolling pin
A baking tray
A selection of festive cutters

1. Put all the ingredients into a bowl, mix them all together, then roll them into a ball.
2. Roll the dough out flat. Then cut out

shapes, like stars and snowmen, with a cutter – and make a little hole in each one so that they can be hung on the tree when they're cooked.

3. Place them on the greased baking tray and ask an adult to pop them in the oven at 180°C/Gas Mark 4 for 20 minutes.

4. When they've cooled, you can paint them bright colours and add some sparkly string.

Christmas Biscuits

You will need
250g plain flour
125g butter
60g caster sugar
A rolling pin
A baking tray
A selection of festive cutters

1. Mix all the ingredients together in a bowl and then slowly knead them together to make a ball.
2. Roll out this pastry until it is about 1cm thick, and then use the festive cookie cutters to cut out angels, stars, Christmas trees and so on.
3. Place them on the greased baking

tray and ask an adult to put them in the oven to cook for 10–15 minutes at 160°C/Gas Mark 3.

4. Let them cool – and enjoy!

Potato-Print Wrapping Paper

Potato-print wrapping paper adds a personal touch to your present-giving – and it's lots of messy fun to make too! You need a shaped cookie cutter and a large potato, or you can press your hands into the paint and use them to make patterns.

1. Cut out a slice from the middle of the potato and press the cookie cutter into it.
2. Then push out the shape you have cut, and dip it into some paint – any colour you like.
3. Press the shape on to a piece of paper, and then repeat to make the coolest wrapping paper around!

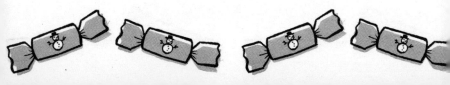

4. You can also place your hands in the paint and then press them against the paper.

Christmas-Tree Paperchain

An easy-to-make decoration to take pride of place in your house.

1. Lay out two pieces of paper, and join them together with some tape.

2. Then fold the paper in half, and then back on itself again so that the paper makes a zigzag shape, like this:

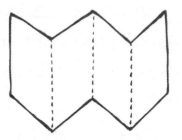

3. Draw a Christmas tree on the first face of the paper, making sure that one set of branches touches both sides of the

paper. This will be the link between the sheets.

4. Then cut out the Christmas-tree shape, taking care not to cut along the folds of the paper.

5. Open out the shape, and you should have a dancing string of trees – which you can decorate with different colours and glitter.

Christmas Hat

Making a festive hat is simple: take a piece of coloured paper, and roll it into a cone shape.

Secure this with tape, and then get decorating – you can use glitter, streamers, and pencils and paint to make it really festive.

Gift Calendar

A perfect present for any family member – you'll need to buy a plain, tear-off calendar.

Stick this to the bottom of a sturdy piece of paper or cardboard, and decorate the background.

You could stick on a photo, or paint handprints, or write a poem and draw pictures around it.

Use some ribbon or string to make a loop to hang it up with.

HAPPY CHRISTMAS

DECEMBER

About the Author

Julia Donaldson is one of the UK's most popular children's writers. Her award-winning books include *What the Ladybird Heard*, *The Detective Dog*, *The Snail and the Whale* and *The Gruffalo*. She has also written many children's plays and songs, and her sell-out shows based on her books and songs are a huge success. She was the Children's Laureate from 2011 to 2013, campaigning for libraries and for deaf children, and creating a website for teachers called picturebookplays.co.uk. Julia and her husband Malcolm divide their time between Sussex and Edinburgh. You can find out more about Julia at www.juliadonaldson.co.uk.

About the Illustrator

Lydia Monks studied Illustration at Kingston University, graduating in 1994 with a first-class degree. She is a former winner of the Smarties Bronze Award for *I Wish I Were a Dog* and has illustrated many books by Julia Donaldson. Her illustrations have been widely admired. You can find out more about Lydia at www.lydiamonks.com.

Have you read

JULIA DONALDSON

Princess Mirror-Belle

TWO BOOKS IN ONE

Illustrated by
LYDIA MONKS

Have you read

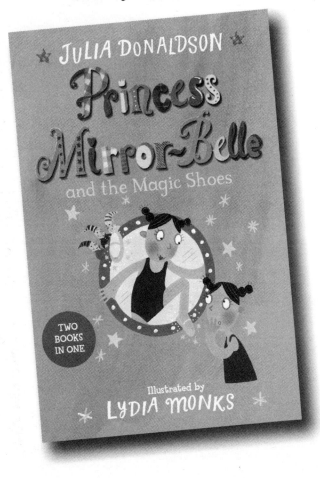

Have you read

JULIA DONALDSON

Princess
Mirror-Belle
and the Flying Horse

TWO BOOKS IN ONE

Illustrated by
LYDIA MONKS

For younger readers

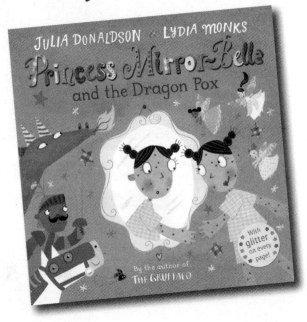